ESCAPE FROM HOTEL INFINITY

Kjartan Poskitt

Quarto is the authority on a wide range of topics.

Quarto educates, entertains and enriches the lives of our readers—enthusiasts and lovers of hands-on living.

www.quartoknows.com

Author: Kjartan Poskitt
Illustrator: Amit Tayal & Sachin Nagar
Consultants: Hilary Koll & Steve Mills
Editor: Amanda Askew
Designer: Punch Bowl Design
QED Editor: Carly Madden

First published in the UK in 2017 by
QED Publishing
Part of The Quarto Group
The Old Brewery
6 Blundell Street
London, N7 9BH

A catalogue record for this book is available from the British Library.

ISBN 978-1-78493-851-2

Printed in China

MIX
Paper from responsible sources
FSC® C016973
www.fsc.org

HOTEL
INFINITY

HOW TO BEGIN YOUR ADVENTURE

Are you ready for a brain-bending mission packed with puzzles and problems?

Then this is the book for you!

Escape From Hotel Infinity isn't like other books where you read through the pages in order. It's a lot more exciting than that because you're the main person in the story! You have to find your own way through the book, flicking backwards and forwards, following the clues until you've finished the whole adventure.

The story starts on page 4, and then tells you where to go next. Every time you face a challenge, you'll have a choice of answers, which look something like this:

A If you think the correct answer is A, GO TO PAGE 23

B If you think the correct answer is B, GO TO PAGE 11

Are you ready?

Then turn the page and let's get started!

Choose the correct answer, and then find the correct page and look for the icon.

Don't worry if you pick the wrong answer. You'll be given an extra clue, then you can go back and try again.

The puzzles and problems in this adventure are all about the wonderful world of numbers, so have your maths skills ready!

To help you there's a list of useful words at the back of the book starting on page 44.

ESCAPE FROM
HOTEL INFINITY

The day starts quietly at Deca University, the world's top facility for national security development.

Suddenly the alarms sound and a message pops up on your computer screen.

ALERT!

Professor Function has been kidnapped! He went to a top-secret conference yesterday and we received this message...

<At hotel. Something strange is going on. Bring help. Be careful.>

Your mission is to find the professor and bring him back. All we have is a map reference, and a helicopter ready to take you there.

You can hear the chopper outside. Are you ready?

 START YOUR QUEST ON PAGE 27.

4

Well done! The 10 dangerous steps are 4, 8, 12, 16, 20, 24, 28, 32, 36 and 40.

You descend the staircase safely and open a door into the waste room.

You decide to avoid the main corridors, so you look for another way out. You'll have to go down one of the chutes.

PRIME WASTE CLEARANCE SYSTEM
TRUE = Laundry   FALSE = Waste Crusher

Prime numbers only divide by themselves and one.

All prime numbers are odd.

Which is the true statement that will lead you to the laundry?

< Prime numbers will only divide by themselves and one.
TUMBLE TO PAGE 18

≥ All prime numbers are odd.
PLUMMET TO PAGE 27

>
Wrong way! Sometimes adding odd numbers can make an even number. For example, 5 + 7 = 12.
TRY AGAIN ON PAGE 26.

6
Not 6 minutes! Remember, each number takes 10 minutes to appear.
GO BACK TO
PAGE 15 AND TRY AGAIN!

You remember that a prime number can only be divided by 1 or itself. Which creeper is safe to climb along?

A
Vine A.
GO TO PAGE 12

B
Vine B.
JUMP TO PAGE 21

C
Vine C.
HEAD TO PAGE 31

Yes, the answer is 7!
4 x 6 + 7 = 31 or 6 x 4 + 7 = 31.

You enter the lift and find only two buttons.

The +5 button will take you up five floors.

The -2 button will take you down two floors.

HOTEL
I N F I N I T Y

+5

-2

Ah, this must be one of the puzzles that the receptionist mentioned.

Clue: You're on floor 0, so if you wanted to get to floor 1, you would need three pushes (+5 -2 -2 = 1).

How many pushes do you need to reach floor 7 from floor 0?

5. RISE TO PAGE 16

4. ELEVATE TO PAGE 37

7. GLIDE UP TO PAGE 26

No! There were 9 grandsons, but you need to count all of the others.
GO BACK TO PAGE 19.

No, this symbol is called PI and it represents the number 3.1416. It is important because if you measure the circumference of any circle and divide it by the diameter, the answer is always PI.
TRY AGAIN ON PAGE 31.

Well done! The orange path is the shortest at just 15 metres in length. (3 + 4 + 3 + 5).

As you reach the computer, ONE turns on the brain-draining helmet.

To save the professor you need to sabotage the computer, but how? All these tough puzzles have given you an idea. Maybe there's a puzzle that would take the computer forever to calculate...

Which set of sums should you put into the computer?

 Start with 100. Keep taking away 2 until you reach zero. GO TO PAGE 16

 Start with 100. Keep dividing by 2 until you reach zero. TURN TO PAGE 23

133

No, basket 133 is dirty! You can test any number by adding the digits together. 1 + 3 + 3 = 7. If the answer divides by 3, then so will the number. But 7 does not divide by 3, so 133 won't divide by 3 either!

TRY AGAIN ON PAGE 18.

7

No, 7 is a **hexagonal** number. If you have 7 counters, you can arrange them in a perfect hexagon shape.

GET BACK TO PAGE 28.

A

This is room 738! Remember when you try to work it out that the lowest numbered door is 734.

HURRY BACK TO THE SAFETY OF PAGE 29.

 740

12

Yes, 12 is a **multiple** of 3, which means it will divide exactly by 3 with no **remainder**.

As you set off down the corridor, the hotel porter appears and demands to know what you're doing.

Er... I'm going to view Professor Function's experiment, but I've forgotten the room number. Can you help?

As you know, everything is a puzzle, so all I can tell you is that it's exactly halfway between room 732 and room 748.

You smile and thank him.

Which room should you be heading for?

738 738. POP TO PAGE 20

741 741. DASH TO PAGE 38

740 740. HURRY TO PAGE 29

No, window 2 is 2 metres wide and the rope only stretches for 3 widths, so the rope will be a little more than 6 metres long.

HAVE ANOTHER TRY ON PAGE 37. **87**

?

No, 32 ÷ 4 = 8, which is not a prime number.

GO BACK TO PAGE 30 AND EXPAND YOUR MIND!

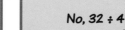

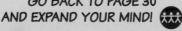

Yes, in just over 4 minutes, the computer system will explode.

The professor waits for you to join him, but ONE has already escaped through the main door, which has closed behind him.

We need another key code! It's the next number in the sequence, but my brain is too tired to think!

DOOR RELEASE
1, 1, 2, 3, 5, 8, 13, 21, ?

1 2 3
4 5 6
7 8 9
0

Can you work out the next number?

△ 30.
FLIP TO PAGE 43

◉ 34.
TURN TO PAGE 32

▣ 42.
GO TO PAGE 18

C

This is room 742 and the door is locked. The next door must be 740.
RUN BACK TO PAGE 29.

740

6

There are six ways to make 10p using only 1p and 2p coins. But using 5ps as well gives you even more ways!
GO BACK TO PAGE 42.

9

A

This creeper has 17 flowers – a prime number.
LET GO AND GET BACK TO PAGE 7.

Yes! Piece 3 goes in the top-right corner.

You quickly fit all of the pieces in place and hide, just as the door opens.

4	3
1	6
2	5

Two nurses leave the room and disappear down the corridor.
Everything is quiet, so you sneak inside.

You've found the professor. His head is wired to a computer.

BRAIN-DRAIN
COUNTDOWN

110-108-104-98-90

A screen shows BRAIN-DRAIN **COUNTDOWN** and a
sequence of numbers that is getting smaller and
smaller! Every ten minutes a new number appears.

50 minutes have
already passed. How
many more minutes
will it be before the
countdown reaches
zero and the professor
is totally drained?

60 60.
DASH TO PAGE 28

80 80.
SNEAK A LOOK AT PAGE 37

6 6.
HEAD TO PAGE 5

Correct! Prime numbers only divide by themselves and 1.

Weeee... PLUMPH!

You drop safely onto a heap of old duvets.

You hear the receptionist giving orders. She's realized you've come to rescue the professor and she isn't pleased!

Search the dirty laundry baskets first! Remember the numbers on them DO NOT divide by three!

Your only option is to hide in the clean basket, but which one is it?

 Basket number 87.
SCRUB UP TO PAGE 37

 Basket number 49.
SPIN OVER TO PAGE 23

 Basket number 133.
TUMBLE ALONG TO PAGE 9

14

No! If you divide 14 by 3, you get 4 2/3, which is a **fraction**, not a whole number.
THINK AGAIN ON PAGE 39.

▢

Not 42! Check to see how much each number is bigger than the last one.
HAVE ANOTHER GO ON PAGE 12.

10 When you answer 'ten ways', the professor smiles slightly before challenging you to another question.

Question two: my great grandfather had three sons, and they each gave him three grandsons, and each grandson gave him three great-grandsons. So how many people is that altogether?

GREAT GRANDFATHER

GREAT-GRANDSONS

What do you say?

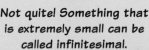 40.
GO TO PAGE 30

27.
FLIP TO PAGE 42

9.
HEAD OVER TO PAGE 8

Not quite! Something that is extremely small can be called infinitesimal.
GO BACK TO PAGE 27.

Try again! This symbol is the Greek letter called Sigma. It means to make a sum or add everything up.
HAVE ANOTHER GO ON PAGE 31. **C**

2 Yes, there are 24 different possible ways to put the digits in order. You know this by using the calculation $4 \times 3 \times 2 \times 1 = 24$.

We'll test the **combinations** one by one, but we need a system so we don't repeat ourselves.

You arrange the digits to make the smallest number, then the next number up, and so on.

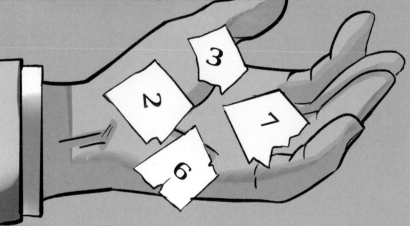

What is the combination?

A 3762.
SHUFFLE ALONG TO PAGE 41

B 2637.
TURN TO PAGE 38

C 6732.
FLIP OVER TO PAGE 28

The professor tries the combination 2367, then 2376... and on the third try, the lock clicks open.

738

Oops! 738 is 6 doors away from 732, but 10 doors away from 748.
GO BACK TO PAGE 10 AND TRY AGAIN! **12**

No! If you add the odd numbers, then take away the even numbers, you don't get 17.
HAVE ANOTHER GO ON PAGE 33.

Well done! The shortest path is 2-17-43-67-51-150-82-90-3-76-104-19-85-56-119-71-5-138-35-42.

You reach the other side just in time to see a lift door closing.

You'll have to reset the lift to stop it, so you prise off a metal panel on the wall.

TO DISABLE LIFT,
PUSH THREE BUTTONS
ADDING UP TO 30.

3 7 8
13 19

Which buttons should you NOT touch?

X [3] and [19] ?
GO TO PAGE 36

! [7] and [13] ?
GO TO PAGE 33

⊘ [8] and [13] ?
GO TO PAGE 26

+
Not 4! The calculation would make 46, not 31.
TRY AGAIN ON PAGE 40.

13
No. Look at how many times 4 goes into 41.
CLIMB BACK TO PAGE 38.

B
No, this creeper has 23 flowers – a prime number.
GO BACK TO PAGE 7.

Yes, window 1 has 7 sections of rope going across – a total of at least 7 metres, which is longer than the other piece of rope.

You tie one end of the rope to the window catch and get ready to throw out the rope.

1 metre below you is a ledge.

2 metres below that is a second ledge.

Beyond that are more ledges and the gap between them doubles each time.

Which is the lowest ledge you can reach with 7 metres of rope?

3↓
The third ledge below the window.
GO TO PAGE 6

4↓
The fourth ledge below the window.
TURN TO PAGE 33

÷2 If the computer starts with 100 and keeps dividing by 2, after 50 sums it will reach 0.0000000000000888, which is very small, but the computer still needs to keep dividing...

Victory! The computer system shuts down and the room falls dark, until an alarm flashes!

DANGER!
OVERHEATING IMMINENT!
KEEP TEMPERATURE
BELOW 65°C!

ONE runs towards the exit. The professor quickly removes the brain-draining helmet and sinks to the floor.

+80°C	+176°F	DANGER!
		+65°C
+60°C	+140°F	OVERHEATING LIMIT
+40°C	+104°F	
+20°C	+60°F	
0°C	32°F	
		-17°C
-20°C	-4°F	CURRENT TEMPERATURE
-40°C	-40°F	

The temperature rises 20°C every minute. How long have you got to leave the room before the system becomes dangerous?

 At least 4 minutes.
GO TO PAGE 12

 At least 5 minutes.
JUMP TO PAGE 41

 At least 6 minutes.
HEAD TO PAGE 27

49
No! This must be a dirty basket because 49 will only divide by 7, not 3.
GO BACK TO PAGE 18.

=
Try again! 20 ÷ 2 = 10, which is not a prime number.
TRY AGAIN ON PAGE 30.

—
No, 40 does not divide by 6.
TRY AGAIN ON PAGE 43.

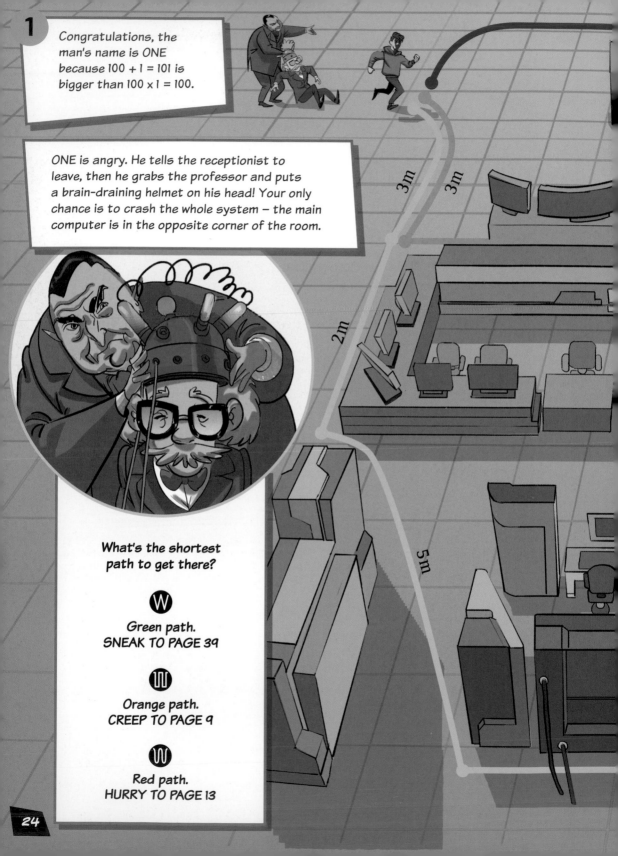

1

Congratulations, the man's name is ONE because 100 + 1 = 101 is bigger than 100 x 1 = 100.

ONE is angry. He tells the receptionist to leave, then he grabs the professor and puts a brain-draining helmet on his head! Your only chance is to crash the whole system — the main computer is in the opposite corner of the room.

3m

3m

2m

5m

What's the shortest path to get there?

W

Green path.
SNEAK TO PAGE 39

III

Orange path.
CREEP TO PAGE 9

W

Red path.
HURRY TO PAGE 13

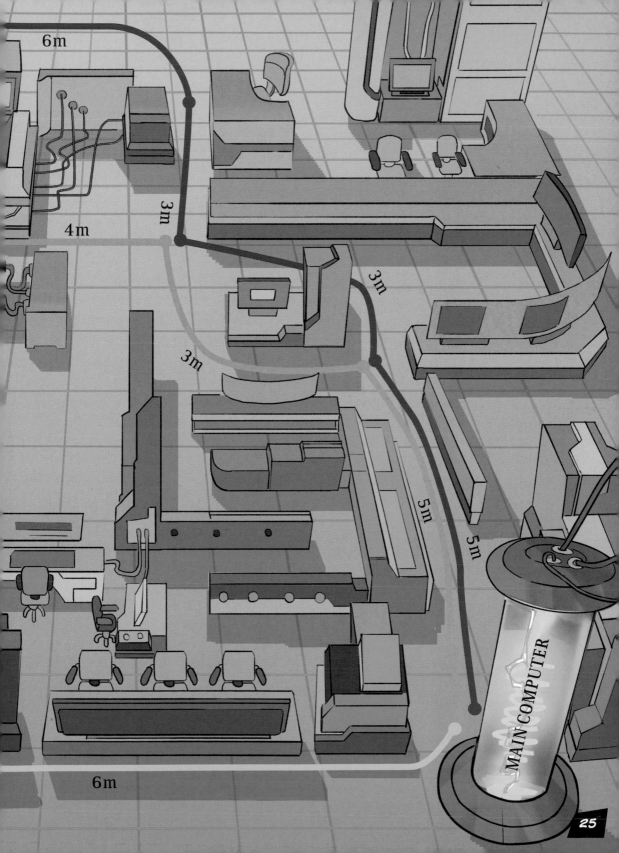

6m

4m

3m

3m

3m

3m

5m

5m

5m

6m

MAIN COMPUTER

7 Well done! Seven pushes brought you to floor 7 (Calculation: +5 −2 −2 +5 −2 −2 + 5 = 7).

You step out of the lift into a long corridor that stretches far in both directions. Opposite the lift are two arrows.

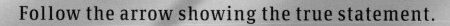

Follow the arrow showing the true statement.

If you **add EVEN** numbers you can never make an **ODD** number.

If you add ODD numbers, you can never make an EVEN number.

$\longleftarrow$ $\qquad$ $\longrightarrow$

HOTEL
I N F I N I T Y

Which arrow do you follow?

 Left. HURRY TO PAGE 43

Right. SNEAK TO PAGE 5

No! There would be six ways to put them in order if there were just three digits. You can work this out by looking at 3 x 2 x 1 = 6.

GO BACK TO PAGE 36 AND THINK AGAIN.

Incorrect! If you push the other three buttons, you get 29.

TRY AGAIN ON PAGE 21.

The helicopter drops you at the edge of a dark forest. Through the trees, you see a gigantic building.

HOTEL INFINITY

As you approach, a man appears.

State your business.

You tell him you're a professor, and late for the top-secret conference.

Professor Point, isn't it? We've been expecting you. Answer the entry question first – what does infinite mean?

What do you say?

Something that goes on forever.
STEP UP TO PAGE 40

Something extremely small.
SNEAK OVER TO PAGE 19

Incorrect! Remember, 2 will only divide by itself and 1, so it IS a prime number, and also even.
GET BACK TO PAGE 5.

6:0

Argh! In 6 minutes the computer would be +103°C and close to exploding!
TRY AGAIN ON PAGE 23.

The porter is SIX – you can see this by counting how many blocks make up the shape.
GO BACK TO PAGE 17.

Yes, there are just 60 minutes left. The sequence goes 110–108–104–98–90–80–68–54–38–20–0.

So after six more lots of 10 minutes, the countdown will reach zero! You need to stop the experiment.

There are three numbered buttons. The numbers represent different shapes, and there is a key to show what they do.

EXPERIMENT CONTROLS

 NUMBER = STOP EXPERIMENT

 NUMBER = ALARM

▲ **NUMBER = ROOM DESTRUCT**

7   9   10

You're looking for a **square number**, but which one is it? Time is ticking, so don't push the wrong button!

Which button shows a *square* number?

10 10.
GO TO PAGE 31

9 9.
TURN TO PAGE 42

7 7.
FLIP TO PAGE 9

No, 6732 is far too high.
HAVE ANOTHER
TRY ON PAGE 20.

KAZZAK! Did you step on tile 121? That's a square number because 11 x 11 = 121.
GO BACK TO PAGE 32.

Yes! You set off to room 740, which is exactly 8 doors away from both 732 and 748.

Oh no! A lot of the door numbers have fallen off. The rooms on this side of the corridor are all even numbers.

Which is the door to room 740?

A Door A.
GO TO PAGE 9

B Door B.
STEP ALONG TO PAGE 41

C Door C.
FLIP TO PAGE 12

Yes! There was 1 great grandfather, 3 sons, 3 x 3 = 9 grandsons and 3 x 3 x 3 = 27 grandsons, so 1 + 3 + 9 + 27 = 40.

You're doing well, but I have one final question, and this is a tricky one! Which of these calculations results in a **prime number**?

$39 \div 3$

$20 \div 2$

$32 \div 4$

The professor scribbles some sums on a pad. What do you answer?

39 ÷ 3.
CHECK ON PAGE 16

20 ÷ 2.
TURN TO PAGE 23

32 ÷ 4.
SAUNTER TO PAGE 10

If you put piece 4 in the top-right corner, then you'll need to put one odd piece on top of another – which is wrong!

HAVE ANOTHER THINK AND GO BACK TO PAGE 41. Ⓑ

100

No! 100 + 100 is only 200, which is a lot smaller than 100 x 100 = 10,000.

GO BACK TO PAGE 11 AND HAVE ANOTHER SHOT. ∞

C

This plant has 18 flowers and as 2 x 9 = 18, the number 18 is not prime and you're safe!

You climb along the creeper and in through a window.

This library must belong to the Infinity Project. The control room is nearby, but where is the entrance?

Hmm, I've got an idea! Look for something to do with infinity...

You see three books with strange symbols on the back. Which one represents infinity?

π π GO TO PAGE 8

∞ ∞ HEAD TO PAGE 11

Σ Σ JUMP TO PAGE 19

16

If you divide 16 by 3, you'll end up with 5 1/3, which isn't a whole number!
TRY AGAIN ON PAGE 39.

10

ARGHHH! This button will make the room self-destruct and destroy everything inside it! 10 is a triangle number. If you have 10 counters, you can arrange them in a perfect triangle shape.
DASH BACK TO PAGE 28. **60**

Yes! You add together two numbers to get the next one. These numbers are called the **Fibonacci Series**.

You enter code 34 and the door opens to a room with a tiled floor.

ONE is standing at the far end and has just clicked a large switch.

Stop!

The square-numbered tiles are electrified and you cannot step diagonally!

2 START	17	43	28	61
33	64	67	107	8
36	150	51	77	100
90	82	9	144	80
3	16	119	71	5
76	4	56	25	138
104	19	85	49	35
47	62	121	11	42

Oh no! You'd better tread carefully.

Can you find a safe way across the tiles by NOT stepping on square numbers or stepping diagonally? Take your time...

What is the smallest number of tiles you step on to reach the door?

20 tiles.
STEP TO PAGE 21

15 tiles.
GO TO PAGE 39

14 tiles.
TURN TO PAGE 28

! Correct! You push 3, 8 and 19 together and the lift grinds to a halt, just as the receptionist appears and demands to know what's going on.

She looks shocked and offers you her phone. You pull a card from your pocket – a secret hotline for emergencies only.

I'm from Deca University. I'm afraid the Infinity Project Leader is a criminal. I need to call our Security HQ to pick him up.

ADD THE ODD NUMBERS TOGETHER. ADD THE EVEN NUMBERS TOGETHER. TAKE AWAY THE LOWEST FROM THE HIGHEST.

2 9 7 4
8 4 5 7
7 6 3 5
6 1 2 1

What is the hotline number?

15.
GO TO PAGE 38

13.
GO TO PAGE 17

17.
GO TO PAGE 20

4↓

Oops! The fourth ledge is 1 + 2 + 4 + 8 = 15 metres below the window. The rope isn't long enough!

GO BACK TO PAGE 22.

🔒3

No! 7632 is the biggest number you can make with the four digits, but that's not the question. As there are four digits, the number of different ways you can put them in order is 4 x 3 x 2 x 1.

TRY AGAIN ON PAGE 36.

=

Not 6! The calculation would make 34, not 31.

HAVE ANOTHER GO ON PAGE 40.

Yes, the receptionist is TWELVE – she wears the badge showing twelve blocks. She looks angry as the agent takes her away.

Well done, you've found the professor and shut down Project Infinity!

The professor shows you a door behind a curtain, which leads to a staircase used by the staff. The padlock has a four-**digit** passcode.

You're in luck, for once! Someone has written down the code, then torn it up.

2   3   6   7

How many different ways can you put the four digits in order?

1. 6.
SHUFFLE ALONG TO PAGE 26

2. 24.
TURN TO PAGE 20

3. 7632.
FLIP TO PAGE 33

You quickly work out three possible arrangements – 6723, 3627 and 7326 – but there must be loads.

I
No, 30 can be divided by 5 and 6 (5 x 6 = 30), but not by 4.
HAVE ANOTHER GO ON PAGE 43.

X
No! If you push the other three buttons, you get 28.
GO BACK TO PAGE 21.

Yes! 87 = 29 x 3, so this must be a clean basket.

You both get into the basket and shut the lid until the coast is clear.

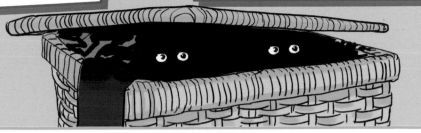

At the back of the room are windows – your only way out – with shutters held in place by ropes.

Which length of rope is longest, so you could use it to climb out safely?

 Window 1 is 1 **metre** wide, so the rope is longer.
TURN TO PAGE 22

 Window 2 is 2 metres wide, so the rope is longer.
OVER TO PAGE 10

4

That's incorrect!
Four pushes could take you to floor 20, 13 or 6.
HAVE ANOTHER GO ON PAGE 8.

80

Not 80 minutes! The first number is 110. You take away 2 to get 108. Then take away 4 to get 104, then take away 6, then take away 8 and so on... until you reach zero. How many more numbers do you need to count down?
TRY AGAIN ON PAGE 15.

Congratulations, 2637 opens the padlock. There is a sign on the wall just inside the door.

You look at a long staircase that descends into darkness...

DANGER!
There are 41 steps.
All steps that are a multiple of 4 are UNSAFE.

HOTEL
INFINITY

How many dangerous steps are there?

10 10. STUMBLE TO PAGE 5

13 13. STEP DOWN TO PAGE 21

9 9. JUMP TO PAGE 43

741

Think again! 741 is 7 doors away from 748, but 9 doors away from 732.
LOOK AGAIN ON PAGE 10. **12**

Oh dear! 15 is too high. You must've miscounted.
TRY AGAIN ON PAGE 33. **!**

On the screen you see the professor and he's wearing an electrode helmet on his head!

There's something strange going on, for sure. You need to find him – and fast!

You try to open the door, but it has automatically locked. A keypad flashes with a question.

WHICH NUMBER DIVIDES EXACTLY BY 3?

12 14 16

What number do you key in?

12 12. *GO TO PAGE 10*

14 14. *GO TO PAGE 18*

16 16. *GO TO PAGE 31*

ZZZAPPP! Did you step on tile 144? That's a square number because 12 x 12 = 144.
GO BACK TO PAGE 32.

W

The green path is 16 metres long and isn't the shortest route to the main computer.
GO BACK TO PAGE 24 AND TRY AGAIN.

Well done! Infinite means something that goes on and on.

The porter gestures for you to enter. You'd better hurry before the real Professor Point arrives!

The receptionist greets you coldly and explains that you need to watch a recording.

Only the brightest people can take part, so we've set puzzles around the hotel to test you. To start, work out on which floor you will watch the recording.

She hands you a piece of paper.

Put the **numbers** 7, 4, 6 into the **calculation** so that it works. The **Infinity** Project recording is on the floor number before the = sign.

$$\blacksquare \times \blacksquare + \blacksquare = 31$$

HOTEL
INFINITY

Which number goes before the = sign?

❌ 7.
TURN TO PAGE 8

➕ 4.
LOOK AT PAGE 21

🟰 6.
FLIP TO PAGE 33

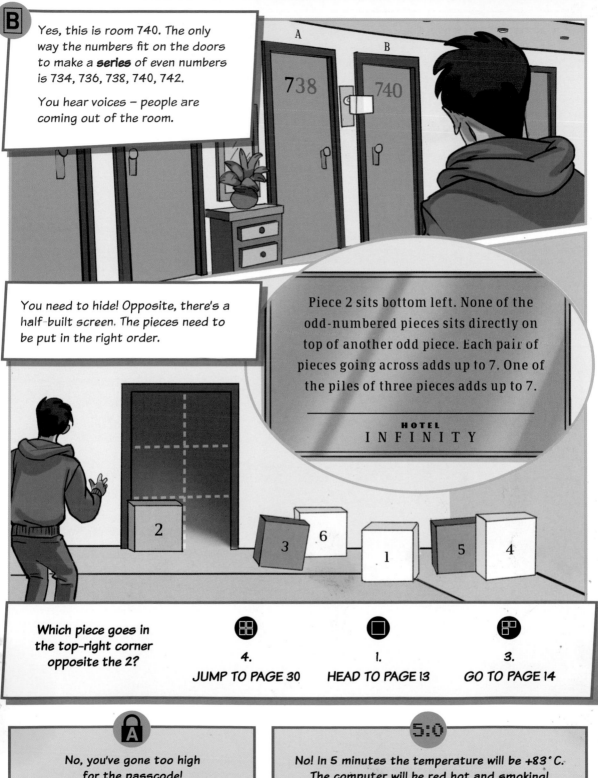

B Yes, this is room 740. The only way the numbers fit on the doors to make a **series** of even numbers is 734, 736, 738, 740, 742.

You hear voices – people are coming out of the room.

A   B
738   740

You need to hide! Opposite, there's a half-built screen. The pieces need to be put in the right order.

Piece 2 sits bottom left. None of the odd-numbered pieces sits directly on top of another odd piece. Each pair of pieces going across adds up to 7. One of the piles of three pieces adds up to 7.

HOTEL
I N F I N I T Y

2   3   6   1   5   4

Which piece goes in the top-right corner opposite the 2?

4.
JUMP TO PAGE 30

1.
HEAD TO PAGE 13

3.
GO TO PAGE 14

No, you've gone too high for the passcode!
GO BACK TO PAGE 20.

No! In 5 minutes the temperature will be +83°C. The computer will be red hot and smoking!
RUSH BACK TO PAGE 23.

The countdown stops. Phew! If you **multiply** any number by itself, you get a square number. As 9 = 3 x 3 then 9 is a square number. Also, if you have a square number of counters, you can arrange them in a perfect square shape.

Hello, Professor! Are you ok? I'm from the university and I'm here to rescue you.

You release the professor's arms and he reaches up and tugs on the electrodes.

You could be tricking me! Answer my security questions first – as per university protocol. Question one: if you had any number of 1p, 2p and 5p coins, how many ways can you make the value **equalling** the name of our university?

Your university is called Deca, meaning ten.
How many ways can you make 10p from 1p, 2p and 5p?

6 6 ways. GO TO PAGE 12

10 10 ways. FLIP TO PAGE 19

No, there were 27 great-grandsons, but what about the others? THINK AGAIN ON PAGE 19. **10**

½

Try again! ½ is not a whole number. HAVE ANOTHER TRY ON PAGE 11 BEFORE HE NOTICES.

Correct! If you add even numbers, you can NEVER make an odd number.

The corridor leads to a small room with Infinity Project on the door.

It's empty except for some headsets. You pick up one to watch the recording.

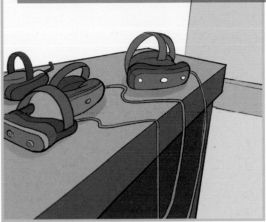

The headset needs to be activated first.

To activate this headset, key in the number that can be **divided** by 4, 5 and 6?

What number do you key in?

40.
GO TO PAGE 23

60.
GO TO PAGE 13

30.
GO TO PAGE 36

 9
Oops, you must have miscounted.
GO BACK TO PAGE 38.

No! In the sequence, you add together two numbers to get the next one. It starts 1 + 1 = 2, then 1 + 2 = 3.
GO BACK TO PAGE 12 AND TRY AGAIN.

GLOSSARY

ADD (+)

In a calculation, the plus sign tells you to add numbers together to find the total. Example: 6 + 7 = 13.

CALCULATION

There are four main types of calculation in maths: addition, subtraction, multiplication and division.

COMBINATION

Two or more things that can be put together. Example: If there are four cubes (red, white, green, yellow) and you can mix any two together, there are six different combinations you can make (red/white, red/green, red/yellow, white/green, white/yellow, green/yellow).

COUNTDOWN

A series of numbers that are getting smaller, usually by counting backwards. For example: 3-2-1-0 or 20-15-10-5-0.

DIGIT

The figures 0, 1, 2, 3, 4, 5, 6, 7, 8, 9 are digits. We use digits to write numbers, in the same way that we use letters to write words.

DIVIDE (÷)

In a calculation, the dividing sign tells you to divide the first number by the second number to find the answer. Example: 8 ÷ 4 = 2.

EQUALS (=)
In a calculation, the equals sign tells you when two things have the same value. Example: 2 + 3 = 5.

ETERNITY
A time that lasts for ever.

EVEN
Any number ending in 0, 2, 4, 6 or 8. Even numbers will always divide exactly by 2.

FIBONACCI SERIES
A sequence of numbers that starts 1, 1, 2, 3, 5, 8, 13, 21. Each number is made from adding the two numbers before it together.

FRACTION
This is what you get when a whole number is divided into equal parts. Example: The decimal 0.7 can be shown as a fraction 7/10.

HEXAGON
Any shape with six straight sides. A regular hexagon has equal sides and equal angles.

INFINITY
A number that goes on forever without ending. If you put 1÷3 into a calculator, the answer starts 0.3333 and the line of threes goes on forever. The number of threes is infinite.

LOWEST COMMON MULTIPLE

The smallest number that two numbers will divide into. Example: 24 is the lowest common multiple of 6 and 8.

METRE

A measurement of length. 1 metre (m) is the same as 100 centimetres (cm).

MULTIPLE

A multiple is a number that can be divided equally by another number. Example: any number that divides by 6 is a multiple of 6. Therefore the first multiples of 6 are 12, 18, 24, 30.

MULTIPLY (X)

In a calculation, the multiplication or times sign tells you to multiply numbers together to find the answer. Example: 9 x 7 = 63.

NUMBER

A number is made up of one or more digits. A number can be positive or negative. For example: 325 is a positive number and –67 is a negative number.

ODD

Any number ending in 1, 3, 5, 7 or 9. If you try to divide an odd number by 2, you will always get 1 left over.

PRIME NUMBER

A prime number will only divide by itself and 1. Example: 24 is not prime because it will divide by 1, 2, 3, 4, 6, 8, 12 and 24. But 23 is prime because it will only divide by 1 or 23.

REMAINDER

If you divide a large number by a small number and the answer isn't exact, the number left over is the remainder. For instance 17 ÷ 3 = 5 with a remainder of 2.

SEQUENCE
See *Series*

SERIES
A set of numbers that follows a pattern. Example: 5, 8, 11, 14, 17 is a series because each number is 3 more than the last one.

SQUARE NUMBER
If you multiply any number by itself you get a square number. Example: 5 x 5 = 25, so 25 is a square number. If you have a square number of counters, you can always arrange them in a perfect square shape.

SUM
If you sum up a set of numbers, you add them all together. The total is called the sum of the numbers.

WHOLE NUMBER
Any number that doesn't have a fraction after it. 10 is a whole number but 10½ or 10.5 is not.

TAKING IT FURTHER

The Maths Quest books are designed to motivate children to develop and apply their maths skills through engaging adventure stories. The stories work as games in which children must solve a series of mathematical problems to progress towards the exciting conclusion.

The books do not follow a conventional pattern. The reader is directed to jump forwards and backwards through the book according to the answers given. If their answers are correct, they progress to the next part of the story; if the answer is incorrect, the reader is directed back to try the problem again. Additional support may be found in the glossary at the back of the book.

TO SUPPORT YOUR CHILD'S MATHEMATICAL DEVELOPMENT YOU CAN:

- Read the book with your child.

- Solve the initial problems and discover how the book works.

- Continue reading with your child until he or she is using the book confidently, following the GO TO instructions to find the next puzzle or explanation.

- Encourage your child to read on alone. Ask 'What's happening now?'. Prompt your child to tell you how the story develops and what problems they have solved.

- Discuss numbers in everyday contexts: working out how much change to expect when shopping, estimating how many steps it takes to walk somewhere, using timetables, telling the time on different clocks, and so on.

- Have fun with number sequences and patterns. Say four numbers in a sequence (e.g. 22, 26, 30, 34) and ask what comes next. Discuss coins: how many ways can you make 7p with 1p, 2p and 5p pieces? Count backwards. List doubles, halves, square numbers and primes.

- Use dice and playing cards in number games with your child.

- Most of all, make maths fun!